Alice Through The Looking-Glass

Lewis Carroll
Adapted by Lesley Sims

Illus...
Mauro ...

Reading Consul... Alison Kelly
Roehampton University

This story is set in an imaginary world that is like a chess board. So, lots of the characters you'll meet are pieces used in the game of chess: a red king and queen, a white king and queen, red and white knights and pawns.

Red knight   White queen   Red pawn   White pawn   Red queen

Contents

Chapter 1

The looking-glass house

"Kitty," said Alice one day, "you look like the Red Queen. Can you play chess?"

Kitty yawned.

Alice held her up to the mirror. "See the looking-glass house Kitty? That's where you'll go if you don't behave."

"Imagine what it's like to live there," she added, dreamily. "Let's pretend the glass has gone soft, so we can get through. Oh!"

4

To her surprise, Alice found herself up on the mantelpiece, with no idea how she got there.

The glass was melting away, like a bright silvery mist. In a moment, Alice was through and had crossed over into the looking-glass room.

Alice sat on the mantelpiece and
stared. A chess board
lay on the floor
and the chess
pieces were
strolling around.

She could see the Red King
and Queen, the White King and
Queen, pawns and knights. But
none of them seemed to see Alice.

Then she spotted a
book. Alice jumped
down and opened it
– but the book was
written in a language
she didn't know.

JABBERWOCKY

'Twas brillig, and the slithy toves
Did gyre and gimble in the wabe:
All mimsy were the borogoves,
And the mome raths outgrabe.

Alice puzzled over this for some time until a thought struck her. "As it's a looking-glass book, perhaps I should hold it up to a mirror..."

And this is what she saw:

JABBERWOCKY

'Twas brillig, and the slithy toves

Did gyre and gimble in the wabe:

All mimsy were the borogroves,

And the mome raths outgrabe.

"Very pretty," she said. She didn't like to admit she still couldn't understand it at all.

"Oh!" she cried, jumping up. "If I don't hurry, I shall have to go back before I've explored anywhere."

She ran from the room and raced down some stairs, almost floating through the hall to the front door.

Chapter 2

A garden of talking flowers

Out in the garden, Alice saw a hill with a path that seemed to lead to it. "I'll see the garden much better from up there," she thought.

But the path had more
twists and turns than a
corkscrew. Whichever way
Alice went, she always
ended back at
the house.

At last, she turned to a flower
waving gracefully in the wind. "Oh
Tiger-lily, I do wish you could talk."

"I can," said the Tiger-lily, "when there's anyone worth talking to."

Alice was so astonished that, for a minute, she couldn't speak herself.

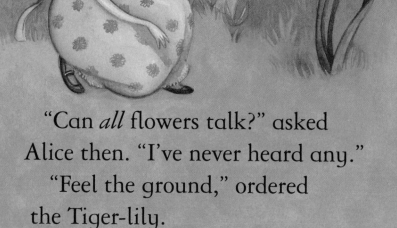

"Can *all* flowers talk?" asked Alice then. "I've never heard any."

"Feel the ground," ordered the Tiger-lily.

"It's very hard," said Alice.

"In most gardens," the Tiger-lily said, "the beds are too soft. All the flowers are asleep."

"I never thought of that," said Alice. "Are there any people in this garden besides me?" she went on.

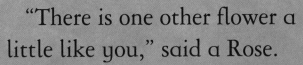

"There is one other flower a little like you," said a Rose.

Alice smiled. Perhaps there was another girl to play with.

"She's coming!" said a Marigold.

Alice looked around eagerly. But it was the Red Queen – and she seemed to have grown. When Alice had last seen her, she was only the size of a thumb. Now, she was taller than Alice.

I think I'll go and meet her.

You can't possibly do that.

"If you want to find her, walk the other way," advised the Rose.

This sounded like nonsense to Alice, so she set off in the Queen's direction.

To her surprise, she lost sight of her in a moment and found herself back at the house.

Alice could still see the Queen, a long way off, so she decided to try

walking in the opposite direction. That worked beautifully. In less than a minute, they were face to face by the hill.

"Where are you going?" asked the Queen.

"I'm not sure," Alice replied. "I keep losing my way."

"*Your* way?" said the Queen. "All the ways around here belong to *me*. But why are you here at all?"

"I wanted to see the garden, your Majesty," said Alice.

The Red Queen patted her on the head, which Alice didn't like at all, and led her up the hill.

From the top you could see
all over the country – and what
a peculiar country it was. The
ground was divided up into squares
by hedges and tiny streams.

It's like a giant
chessboard!

"We're in the Second Square,"
said the Queen. "When you get
to the Eighth Square, you'll be a
Queen. Quick! Run!"

She grabbed Alice's
hand and
they ran.

Faster! Faster!

The strange thing was, they
didn't seem to get anywhere.

"We haven't moved!" Alice panted
when they finally stopped to rest.

"Of course not," said the Queen. "Here, it takes all the running you can do, to stay in the same place. To go somewhere else, you must run at least twice as fast."

Are you thirsty? Have a dry biscuit.

"Now, directions," said the Queen. "A pawn – that's you – goes two squares in its first move. So you'll go very quickly through the Third Square, by railway I should think. In the Fourth Square you'll meet Tweedledum and Tweedledee."

"The Fifth Square has a shop and the Sixth belongs to Humpty Dumpty. The Seventh is forest, but a Knight will show you the way, and in the Eighth Square we shall be Queens together and it's all feasting and fun!"

"Goodbye!" added the Queen, and she vanished.

Chapter 3

The Third Square

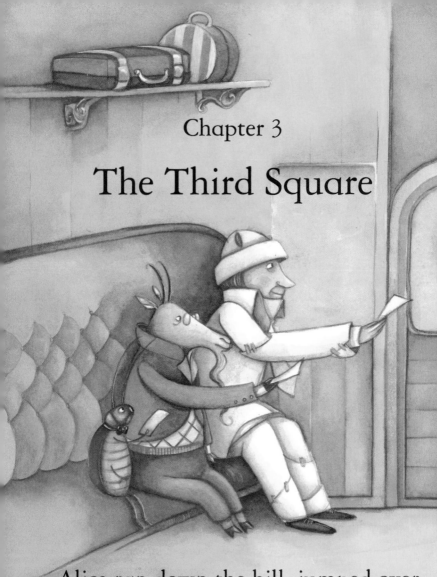

Alice ran down the hill, jumped over a stream to the woods in the Third Square and found herself on a train.

"Tickets please!" said a Guard.
"I'm afraid I haven't got one,"
said Alice.

The Guard
peered at Alice. "You're
going the wrong way," he
announced and went off.

The other passengers glared at Alice. "I don't belong here," she explained. "I was in some woods just now. I wish I could get back."

"You might make a joke about that," said a tiny voice in her ear. "You know, you *wood* if you could."

"Don't tease," said Alice, looking to see where the voice came from.

The little voice sighed deeply, as a shrill scream from the engine made everyone jump.

24

The train gave a lurch and Alice
found herself sitting under a
tree, surrounded by the
strangest insects.

The sighing voice on
the train belonged to
a gnat, who sat on
a twig above her.
It gave another
sigh and seemed
to sigh itself
away.

Alice saw a road leading through the trees and set off. Soon, she came upon two signposts, both pointing the same way.

TO TWEEDLEDUM'S HOUSE →

To The House of TWEEDLEDEE →

"Perhaps they live in the same house," thought Alice. "I shall go and say hello. They might tell me the way out of these woods."

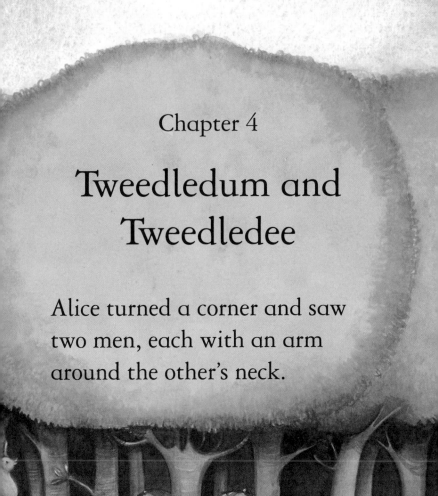

Chapter 4

Tweedledum and Tweedledee

Alice turned a corner and saw two men, each with an arm around the other's neck.

"If you think we're waxworks," said Tweedledum, "you should pay."

"On the other hand," said Tweedledee, "if you think we're alive, you ought to speak."

"I'm sorry," said Alice. "I was wondering how to get out of these woods."

"Do you like poetry?" Tweedledee asked and he began to recite.

The Walrus and the Carpenter

The sun was shining on the sea
Shining with all his might:
He did his very best to make
The billows smooth and bright —
And this was odd, because it was
The middle of the night.

"If it's a very long poem," Alice said politely, "would you please tell me first which road...?"

Tweedledee smiled gently and continued. The poem *was* a long one...*

... 'The time has come,' the Walrus said,
'To talk of many things:
Of shoes—and ships—
and sealing wax—
Of cabbages—and kings—
And why the sea is boiling hot—
And whether pigs have wings.' ...

*It's so long, there's only room for one more verse here. Page 64 has details on where to find the whole poem.

As Tweedledee
finished, a fearsome growling
rattled the trees.

"Are there any lions in these
woods?" Alice asked timidly.

"It's only the Red
King snoring,"
said Tweedledee.

"He's dreaming about you," said
Tweedledum. "If he woke up, you'd
go out – bang! – like a candle."

Alice felt rather upset about this,
though she didn't fully believe it.

"I think I'll go," she said.

Tweedledum grabbed her wrist.
"Look!" he shouted, pointing to a
broken toy on the ground. "That's
my nice new rattle. He's ruined it!
We must have a battle."

The pair vanished
into their house. A minute
later, they came out, with armfuls
of blankets, rugs, saucepans and
and an umbrella.

"I hope you're good at tying
things on," said Tweedledum.

"We'd better hurry," said
Tweedledum. "It's getting dark."

A big black cloud was hovering
ahead. As it came closer, Alice saw
it wasn't a cloud at all.

It was a huge
black crow. With
frightened squeals,
the brothers ran off.

Chapter 5

Wool and water

Alice sheltered under a tree. "I wish the crow wouldn't flap its wings so," she thought. "It's like a hurricane."

A shawl blew into Alice, closely followed by the White Queen.

Alice pinned the shawl back on the White Queen and tried to tidy her hair, which was a terrible mess.

"Would you like to be my maid?" asked the Queen. "Tuppence a week and jam every other day."

Jam tomorrow and jam yesterday, but never jam today.

"I don't think so," said Alice.
"This is such a strange place."
"You'll get used to living
backwards," the Queen said kindly.
"OW! OW!" she suddenly cried out.
"My finger!" Her screams were like
a whistling
steam train.

What is it?
Have you pricked
your finger?

Not yet.
But I soon will.

The Queen tried to straighten her shawl and the brooch flew undone. As she grabbed it, the pin slipped and the Queen pricked her finger. "Well, that explains the bleeding."

"But why don't you scream now?" said Alice, ready to cover her ears.

"Oh, I've done all the screaming already," the Queen replied.

Alice frowned. "It's so hard to believe things here."

"It's just practice," said the Queen. "When I was your age I believed as many as six impossible things before breakfast. Well, I must be off."

Watch your finger!

Oh, it's much be-tter. Be-e-tter! Be-e-ehh!

Alice stared at the Queen, who seemed to have turned into a sheep. And the woods were now a shop.

"May I look around?" asked
Alice. But wherever she looked,
that shelf was empty, though
the others were as full as ever.

"Well, what do you want to
buy?" asked the sheep.

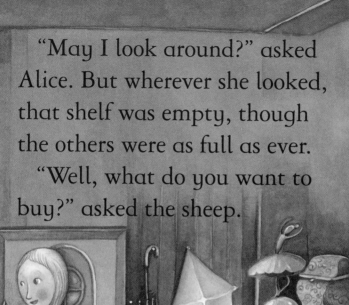

I'd like an
egg, please.

The sheep pointed
to the darkest end
of the shop with a
knitting needle. "Get
an egg from the shelf
over there," she said.

41

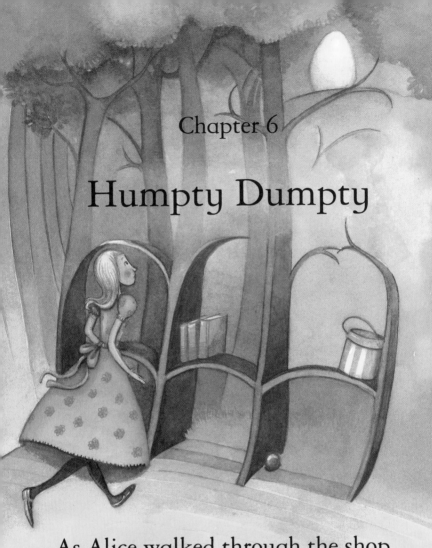

Chapter 6

Humpty Dumpty

As Alice walked through the shop, the shelves turned into trees and she was back in the woods. The egg grew larger and larger until...

"Humpty Dumpty!"
cried Alice, once she was
close enough to see his face.
Softly, she recited:

Humpty Dumpty sat on a wall
Humpty Dumpty had a great fall
All the king's horses
And all the king's men
Couldn't put Humpty together again.

43

Humpty sat, with his legs crossed, on top of a very high, narrow wall.

"Wouldn't you be safer down on the ground?" Alice asked him.

44

"Not at all," said Humpty Dumpty. "Why, if I ever *did* fall off – which there's no chance of – but *if* I did – the king has promised me to...

"Send all his horses and all of his men," finished Alice.

"How do you know?" shouted Humpty Dumpty. "You're a spy!"

"I am not!" said Alice. "It's in a book."

"Ah," said Humpty Dumpty, "that's different."

"What a beautiful belt," Alice said, quickly changing the subject.

"It is very annoying," growled Humpty, "when a person can't tell a belt from a tie. This *tie* was an unbirthday present from the White King and Queen. There's glory."

"I'm not sure what you mean by *glory*," Alice remarked.

"It means whatever I choose it to mean," said Humpty Dumpty. "Words are tricky things. But I can manage 'em. Listen to this poem."

Alice sighed. Everyone seemed
to want to tell her poetry today.
Humpty Dumpty's poem made no
more sense than the others.

...I took a corkscrew from the shelf
I went to wake them up myself
And when I found the door was locked
I pushed and pushed and kicked and knocked
And when I found the door was shut,
I tried to turn the handle, but—

"Is that all?" said Alice.
"That's all," said Humpty
Dumpty. "Goodbye."

Chapter 7

Captured!

"Really," thought Alice, as she jumped over a brook into the next square, "that egg was the most unsatisfactory person I ever met."

"Check!" called a voice. A knight dressed in crimson came galloping up to her.

Got you!

"You're my prisoner–"

"Check!" called another voice. Alice looked around in surprise as a White Knight galloped up and almost tumbled off his horse.

She's my prisoner.

But I've rescued her!

"We'll fight for her," the Red Knight declared.

51

The pair rode wildly, waving their clubs. Sometimes one hit the other, knocking him down. If he missed, he fell off his own horse instead.

The battle ended when they both fell off their horses at the same time and finished up, side by side, on their heads.

When they were upright, they shook hands and the Red Knight galloped off.

"Follow me," said the White Knight. "You have one more brook to cross and you'll be a Queen."

At last, they were at the end of the woods. Alice waved goodbye to the White Knight, ran to the brook and bounded across.

Chapter 8

Queen Alice

She landed on a soft lawn, to find
a golden crown on her head and the
Red Queen and the
White Queen sitting
on either side.

I invite you to
Alice's party.

What
party?

And I
invite you!

The next thing she knew, Alice was entering a large dining hall, full of guests. The Red and White Queens sat at the head of the table with a space for Alice in between.

A waiter set a leg of meat before Alice, who looked at it nervously.

"Let me introduce you – Alice, mutton, mutton, Alice," said the Red Queen.

"May I serve you?" asked Alice. "Certainly not!" said the Red Queen. "It's very rude to cut anyone you've been introduced to. Speech!" she added, poking Alice.

"Look out!" screamed the White Queen. "Something's going to happen!" And it did. The candles exploded. The bottles started flying like birds.

It was complete and utter chaos.

Finally, Alice took hold of the tablecloth and pulled. Plates, dishes, guests and candles came crashing down together in a heap on the floor.

"And as for *you*," Alice said, turning to the Red Queen, but she had shrunk to the size of a doll and was running away. "As for you... I'll shake you into a kitten!"

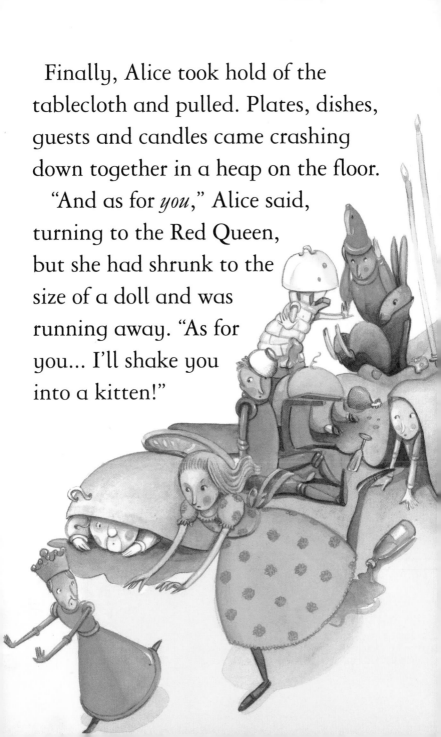

Chapter 9

Shaking

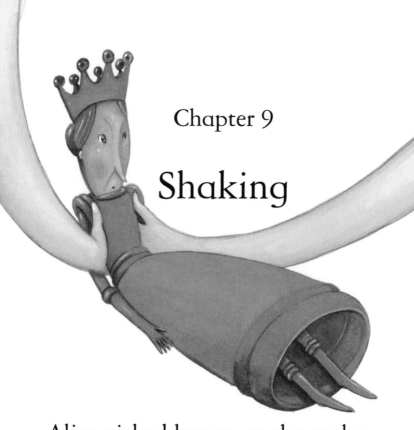

Alice picked her up as she spoke
and shook her back and forth.
The Red Queen didn't say a word,
but her face grew very small, and
her eyes got large and green, and
she kept on growing shorter... and
fatter... and softer... and rounder...

Chapter 10

Waking

...and she really *was* a kitten, after all.

Chapter 11

Who dreamed it?

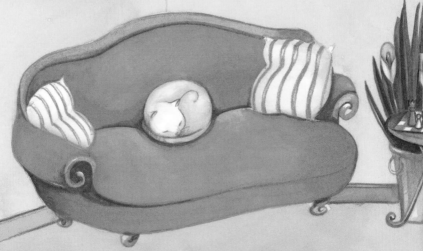

"You shouldn't purr so loudly," said Alice. "You woke me out of such a nice dream. And you've been with me Kitty, all through the looking-glass world, for I'm sure you were the Red Queen."

"The question is," she added, "who *did* dream it? It must have been me or the Red King. He was part of my dream but I was part of his. *Was* it the Red King, Kitty?" Which do *you* think it was?

Lewis Carroll (1832-1898)

Lewis Carroll was the made-up name of Charles Lutwidge Dodgson, a vicar and teacher. His story *Through the Looking-glass and what Alice found there* was published in 1871, a sequel to *Alice's Adventures in Wonderland*.

Internet links

For a translation of the first verse of Jabberwocky and full versions of the poems recited by Tweedledee and Humpty, plus other poems in the original story, go to **www.usborne.com/quicklinks** and type in the keyword 'Alice'.

When using the internet, please follow the internet safety guidelines displayed on the Usborne Quicklinks website.

Designed by Louise Flutter
Series designer: Russell Punter

First published in 2009 by Usborne Publishing Ltd., Usborne House, 83-85 Saffron Hill, London EC1N 8RT, England. www.usborne.com
Copyright © 2009 Usborne Publishing Ltd.